RAVENSBROOKE

HALL

A Tale from Beyond

BARRY DOMINIC GRAHAM
and
HANNAH HELENA GRAHAM

This is a work of fiction.
Names, characters, places, and incidents either
are the product of the author's own imagination or are used fictitiously.
Any resemblance to actual persons, living or dead, events or locales
is entirely coincidental.

ISBN: 9781093589207

EDITED EDITION

Cover art, interior design, editing and layout by
Barry Dominic Graham and Hannah Helena Graham

This book is lovingly and profoundly
dedicated to
Helen Frances Graham…
a wonderful wife and mother,
whom we will love to the end…
of an endless end.

And now here is my secret, a very simple secret:
it is only with the heart that one can see rightly;
what is essential is invisible to the eye.

~ Le Petit Prince ~

ANTOINE DE SAINT-EXUPÉRY
French writer
(1900 ~ 1944)

❦ Contents ❦

Prologue

Amidst the pursuit of any prolonged activity it can be almost inevitable that one can lose sight of original intentions.

When beginning 'Ravensbrooke Hall' we had planned on it being a simple ghost story; however, this was to radically change as we re-evaluated our ideas. There is some fascinating information to be garnered from certain sources which could explain many, if not all, the mysteries of this world and its true origins. We therefore decided to utilise this story as a vehicle through which we could incorporate some of this information.

Novel and novella writing can be a rather sterile business.

During the months whilst being written, the story can be tinged by present-day happenings and the finished product can be quite different to the original tone.

We ultimately found ourselves gazing through a different window at a much more misty and mysterious landscape.

BARRY DOMINIC GRAHAM
and
HANNAH HELENA GRAHAM

NIHIL ALIUD EST QUAM VERITATIS

(NOTHING IS HIGHER THAN TRUTH)

Introduction

Ravensbrooke Hall lies empty.

It has been looking more derelict with every passing year... since being abandoned; gathering layers of dust, ivy and cobwebs, while the owner, Sir Sébastien de Ravensbrooke, travels alone abroad... or so it is believed.

Sir Sébastien is known as a mountaineer, chess master, artist, yogi, social provocateur, occultist, drug addict and libertine.
The locals accused him of being a 'black magician', but this is inaccurate... for in truth, what he actually is, would defy description, belief and comprehension.
Ravensbrooke Hall holds an astounding and unspeakable secret.
The key to heaven and hell.
A gateway to forbidden knowledge.
A portal... to eternity.

Gateway to Ravensbrooke Hall

There are more things in heaven and earth, Horatio,

than are dreamt of in your philosophy.

~ Hamlet ~

WILLIAM SHAKESPEARE
English poet, playwright and actor
1564 ~ 1616

Ravensbrooke Hall

PART ONE

THE QUEST

It is December 5th, 2011.

Almost a decade has passed since Jonathan Swan wrote his last novel. Devoid of ideas and inspiration resulting from ever-growing feelings of disillusionment and despair, he felt defeated by the weight of the world around him and burdened by the shackles and torments of his own mind. Abandoned and betrayed by so very many whom he had trusted and loved, life had become a grey and desolate promontory.

Desperate to rekindle the fires of hope, impetus and imagination which had once burned so strong and brightly within him, he depleted his once abundant finances by scouring the country endeavouring to regain that spark of creativity… and locate the muse which had for so long eluded him.

After driving up from Wotton-under-Edge in Gloucestershire, he approached a small village in the north of Scotland; curiously named, *Cercius* (meaning 'A violent wind blowing in').

This village appeared to have remained unchanged for centuries.

Exhausted, he resigned himself to search for accommodation. Amidst the increasingly dusky twilight, he soon spotted a dim glow of light emanating from a small tavern just ahead of him.

As he drew in to park in front of this antiquated little building with its thatched roof and contorted stone walls, he could now see the classic 'olde-worlde' swinging wooden signage which adorned its entrance.

The sign read… 'The Archon Gate'.

Exiting his treasured 1966 Lamborghini Miura, he briefly examined the tavern's exterior before tentatively entering.

The initial dull murmur of voices suddenly gave way to silence as he opened the door.

The tavern was populated by a ruddy complexioned middle-aged innkeeper sporting a large black moustache... and several elderly men. Two were playing chess at a table and one was sitting observing from the bar.

Jonathan was immediately struck by their look of leanness and poverty; plus the somewhat unsavoury quality they exuded: inbred and somehow sullen.

Made uncomfortable by the dead silence and strange attention, he cautiously made his way to the bar as unfriendly stares followed his every step.

He focused on the fixed gaze and expressionless visage of the innkeeper.

"What can I do for you?" the innkeeper asked in a gruff monotone voice. Pausing for a moment, his mouth becoming dry, Jonathan replied,

"Yes, eh, yes... I, eh... I'm looking for accommodation and was hoping you might know of somewhere nearby?"

"Nothin' round here friend... nothin' at all. You'd best try the next village, Ananias... about ten miles north of here," he answered brusquely.

"Oh... right... I see... well, thanks anyway," Jonathan politely responded whilst steadily backing towards the door.

Upon relievedly exiting this unwelcoming venue, he was then greeted by a violent downpour of freezing rain.

He raced quickly to his car and anxiously recommenced his search.

Somewhat bewildered and becoming rather desperate, he drove north as advised; despite the ungracious delivery of the information he'd received.

Night had now truly fallen.

Complete darkness seemed to descend as quickly as one might blow out a candle; ushering in an ominous cloudy canopy of the blackest pitch.

Shortly after leaving the village, he was soon confronted with a fork in the road ahead.

With windshield wipers frantically sweeping back and forth, being barely effective against the raging torrent, Jonathan struggled desperately to see his best option.

He chose left.

Several miles later, having been travelling along an uneven and obviously

unmaintained road through dense dark forest, he was able to see ahead...
on his left... an old stone-pillared gateway, somewhat disturbingly
surmounted by impressively carved golden eagles.

Thinking this may be a valid possibility for temporary shelter, he
turned accordingly towards this ancient looking, elaborately ornate
entrance; momentarily pausing before journeying onwards down a long,
seemingly endless, equally unkempt driveway.

Eventually, the gradually increasing outline of a huge unlit building
emerged dark and baleful before him.

As he drew close to what appeared to be the entrance to this towering,
umbrageously gloomy edifice, he brought his vehicle to a smooth
standstill and stepped out onto a mossy cobblestoned forecourt.

The rain had now subsided... with the onyx clouds surrendering to the
ghostly glow of a new moon; evoking the illusion of unearthly stillness...
despite the penetration of this bleak and foreboding scene by the
cacophonic, distinct and unmistakeable, deep harsh croak of numerous,
unseen, ravens!

These crepuscular creatures seemed to inhabit every louring branch,
ridge and crevice.

Peculiarly, a vague scent of lavender permeated the air... borne faintly
on a gentle, but chilling breeze.

As his senses heightened, he became conscious that this imposing and
incredible 'mise en scène' was already imprinting and embedding itself
deep into his soul and imagination.

The building was both archaic and eclectic.

The wind suddenly increased: wuthering round the corners and in the
chimneys of the old mansion, as it stood silhouetted... imposing and
eerie in the pale moonlight.

The property appeared broken-down and crumbling.

Stones and rubble lay strewn around its foliage covered base... with ivy
tenderly caressing its walls: winding and creeping its way evermore
heavenwards.

Amidst an adjacent wooded area, he could just about make out what
appeared to be the ruined remains of a smaller structure.

As his eyes progressively adjusted to the darkness, he could see that this
had probably been some old chapel... probably monastic in origin.

Beside it was a small cemetery encompassed by the remnants of a
timeworn wall.

The gravestones, startlingly, could be seen with creepy clarity... with their lichen veneer quasi-incandescent beneath the meniscus moon.

Suddenly, Jonathan became, inexplicably, engulfed and overwhelmed by fear as he turned and caught sight of the enormous oak doors, which loomed malevolently in the distance.

His flesh began to creep as he apprehensively and irresolutely approached them.

With his heart pounding like a blacksmith's hammer on an anvil... gripped by the fear of awful expectation... he reached the ominous murky threshold of this ostensibly forsaken mansion house.

PART TWO

~ A SPECTRAL EVENING ~

The enormous doors were shrouded beneath a darkened arcane porch.

Etched in the stone above the entrance was an emblazoned family coat of arms adorned atop by a raven; displaying beneath its escutcheon, the name 'de Ravensbrooke'.

Further down, in bold decorative capitals, was also inscribed a Latin motto, which read: 'NIHIL ALIUD EST QUAM VERITATIS' (translating as 'Nothing is higher than truth').

On each of the doors was a black iron door knocker designed like a gargoyle's head holding a thick ring of fire between its teeth.

As he stretched out his hand towards one of the huge grotesque effigies, Jonathan had never before felt such a profound feeling of trepidation.

What ominous consequence lay in wait he wondered; now visibly trembling with fear and cold.

Taking one final look over his shoulder, he inhaled deeply, gripped the heavy iron ring and knocked three times then quickly stepped back; waiting in sombre anticipation.

After a minute or so, he repeated the process; this time knocking five times.

He waited.

Still no answer or internal noise.

Upon motioning for a third attempt, the door on the left torpidly creaked open.

As the door begrudgingly groaned ajar, a musty dank odour besieged his senses.

The house was in deep, dark silence; except for intermittent creaks, moans and the raven caws from around and beyond its walls.
After several seconds, he unenthusiastically and hesitantly entered.

Black and brown mould dotted the ceiling in damp clusters, clearly evident of rain seeping through the roof.
He cautiously crossed the threshold of the silent, gloomy vestibule.
All visible windows were covered with grime and dirt.
The tortured December moonlight struggled to penetrate the darkness in fine threaded rays, whilst indistinct shadows surrounded him.
He could see chairs overturned amidst the dust and cobwebs.
Wallpaper lay curled on the floor.
A large jagged hole dug through the wall stood as though daring any to enter.
Picture frames hung askew.
A misplaced grand bookcase stood in the corner of the room, appearing undisturbed for aeons.
The mansion's walls showed black decay... caused by prolonged neglect, with glimpses of original paint hinting at the home's former prosperity.
The entire structure appeared monstrously immense.
A prodigious, once beautiful, staircase swept upward toward unseeable oblivion.
As Jonathan stood thunderstruck with wide-eyed gaze, simultaneously terrified and transfixed by the pageant of disturbing sights, a rush of icy air suddenly surged against him, violently slamming shut the door at his back.
His imagination immediately became violently inflamed.
He could all but see an hysterically screeching wizened spectre race maniacally towards him from the shadows, with gnarled outstretched grasping claws... frantically glaring, bulging, demonic red eyes and tendrils of Medusa-like grey hair streaming and writhing in its wake.

As if by some beautifully timed divine intervention... within a burst of blinding golden white light, a nebulous figure began to form, emerging from the excavated hole in the wall.
All the fear was gone as Jonathan, in this mesmerising moment, observed in amazement the wondrous apparition manifesting before him.
Synchronously, the interior of the hall began to transform back into its original pristine, glorious and lived-in state.
The light gradually dissipated until revealing in crystal clarity an

immaculately dressed gentleman, with a greying black beard and thick, lustrous, swept-back silver hair.

"*I've been waiting for you Jonathan,*" announced the figure in a deep, calm and soothing masculine tone.

"*Waiting for ME... how is that even possible... who... what... ARE you?*" replied Jonathan, reeling with surreal curiosity and abject confusion.

"*I am... at this present moment that is... Sébastien de Ravensbrooke... Sir Sébastien de Ravensbrooke, if you prefer token formality,*" he said facetiously, with a warm smile.

"*At this present moment... what does that even mean... a riddle?... WHAT'S HAPPENING HERE?*" Jonathan exasperatedly beseeched.

"*Please calm yourself... I understand that this must be a somewhat shocking experience for you... therefore... please... just allow me to elaborate a little for you.*" Jonathan forced himself to withhold any further interjection and, with precise facial expression, frustratedly invited his host to continue.

"*As I said... I am known as Sir Sébastien de Ravensbrooke... and was born in this house fifty-seven years ago. I inherited ownership of the estate when my parents tragically died in a small aircraft crash amidst the jungle of the Malay Archipelago... six years past. Due to this I immediately became insular and anti-social. My privileged halcyon days had ended. I searched in vain for solace through alcohol, drugs, sex... and... ultimately, due to the failure of all else... proceeded to delve into the occult arts which, unfortunately, resulted in the local community regarding me as an Aleister Crowleyesque type character... and not without good reason. Despite not adhering to all the fundamental requirements, I actually attempted the elaborate and exhausting Abra-Melin ritual which Crowley himself had failed to complete at Boleskine House, near Loch Ness, in Scotland. A long story short... I was literally rescued from a potentially devastating situation thanks to a fifth dimensional intervention by a race known as the Golden Ones... or Arcturians.*"

"*Rescued... rescued from what?*" asked Jonathan.

"*Rescued from MYSELF essentially,*" replied Sir Sébastien, exhibiting an expression of both fearful sincerity and gratitude.

"*I'm sorry... please... continue... as I'm now about as bewildered as I ever wish to be!*" Jonathan responded dryly, on a long exhaled breath.

"*Although unaware of it at the time... I had put myself... and others... in dreadful danger, by almost opening a dimensional portal to lower fourth density chthonic entities... what MOST refer to as... demons!*"

"*DEMONS!*" exclaimed Jonathan sceptically.

"*Yes... most certainly YES! If it were not for the Golden Ones interceding on my behalf then, literally, all hell would have broken loose!"* **answered Sir Sébastien with absolute conviction.**

"What has all of this insanity got to do with ME... WHAT?" **vociferated Jonathan indignantly.**

"Please listen Jonathan... please," **patiently implored Sir Sébastien.**

"FINE... fine... I'm listening!" **barked Jonathan.**

"Although you may not now recall... WE are Spiritual brothers. We were predestined to meet at this time and place!"

"WHAT... in a derelict mansion house?" **Jonathan wryly remarked, sarcastically.**

Sir Sébastien smiled and briefly chuckled.

"Yes... sounds rather peculiar I know... but it was necessary for me to appear to disappear... and lead the local population to believe that I was travelling abroad... indefinitely. Thus, Ravensbrooke Hall, on this particular dimension, sadly deteriorated in consequence of this."

"Where are you living now then?... how are you living?... BROTHERS?... and why hasn't this place been squatted in or vandalised?" **yawped Jonathan, still deeply perturbed.**

"Firstly Jonathan, this house is profoundly protected... not least, by the force which is embodied by our multitudinous black-feathered friends out there. Secondly, and more importantly... I no longer inhabit this third dimension Jonathan. I was assisted in dimensionally transcending this plane. In simplistic terms, it is rather like this... individually acquired personality and individual learning play a greater role here in third density. Humans are divided into pre-Adamics, who share a species-like Soul pool... and Adamics, who have an individuated Soul. The specific lesson of third density is however, making a choice of orientation of service... towards service-to-others in its greatest possible manifestation, or, service-to-self in its greatest possible manifestation. Making such a conscious choice requires having an individuated Soul and numerous lifetimes in third density for the Soul to acquire its polarity. Fourth density is a partly physical state, where graduates of third density may deepen and perfect their chosen polarity. STS (service-to-self) and STO (service-to-others) groups are distinct in fourth density and do not automatically come in contact... unless in the context of interacting with third density. Most of the UFO phenomenon involves fourth density service-to-self beings. Pure service-to-self may not occur past the fourth level of density, presumably because this is the last and least partly material density. Fourth density beings enjoy more conscious control over physicality and generally form groups, telepathically sharing a common pool of experience while retaining a certain individuality. Souls ranging up to fourth density find themselves in fifth density

between incarnations. This is a contemplation zone where these Souls may observe their past and future lives from a purely ethereal state of being. However, for progress to be realised, Souls must incarnate in the density which best corresponds to their level of progress. Sixth density corresponds to the level of names of God or unified thought forms. Service-to-others entities who no longer need to reincarnate... occupy this level. This corresponds to Angels or Dhyanic beings in other terminologies;... and seventh density is the level where ALL is one and one is All... in a practical, real and meaningful sense. There is no longer any difference between thought and reality... and this corresponds to the notions of the all encompassing God or universe. Demons are, in fact, fourth density STS (service-to-self) *beings... existing at a level superior to the human level... and manipulating humanity and other similar life-forms for their own ends. These are the architects and ultimate controllers of the Matrix... the Archons of darkness... known as such to the Gnostics. We are not talking about strictly ethereal entities. They can appear as solid physical bodies. These are however not native to physicality as experienced by humans. They occupy a realm with variable physicality... and can project themselves into physicality, as experienced by humans, through use of technology or psychic power. The idea of these beings as a human-like life-form from some other planet is misleading. The various strange anomalies, such as variations in the rate of passage of time, spaces being larger on the inside than outside and such effects suggest that these beings experience different laws of physics from that of which we are used to. People can be transported into this different level of reality and temporarily exist there in physical form. Different biological types of beings exist in this context... such as the so-called Grey alien, a somewhat humanoid, four foot tall creature, with large black eyes and a bulb shaped head... plus other forms which include Draco reptilians... Nordic looking humans... and insect-like entities. Although appearing as solid beings... they can walk through walls and materialise from thin air... as they possess an inherent mastery of physicality, whether through technology or by intrinsic ability!"*

Jonathan abruptly interjected.

"Dear God mate... PLEASE stop... my brains are scrambled... this is a bloody NIGHTMARE!" **he cried out pitifully.**

"Forgive me Jonathan... too much too soon perhaps," **replied Sir Sébastien, bowing his head in apparent subtle shame.**

"Let's just get back to WHY you and I are here at this time... and WHY all this craziness was supposedly destined!" **whimpered Jonathan.**

"Alright then... certainly. Since time is merely one of many grand illusions... that imaginary clock which hovers over nature in blithe autonomy... and reality being equally illusory...

my awareness of your ultimate arrival was as predictable as it was inevitable. In simple terms, we WERE destined to meet Jonathan... by YOUR choice in fact. The frozen timescape of relativity theory has enormous holes in it... black holes to be exact. That is because time is warped by gravity. The stronger the gravitational field... the slower the clock hands move. For example, if you live on the ground-floor, you age a little less rapidly than those on higher floors. The effect would be a lot more noticeable if you were pulled into a black hole... where the gravitational warpage of time is infinite. Quite literally, black holes are gateways to the end of time... to nowhen!".

"I don't understand what you're telling me," **pleaded Jonathan.**

"Please... firstly, try and relax your mind a little... and I'll endeavour to explain further. In third-dimensional conditions, celestial amnesia is a common and necessary affliction. The Divine law of Free Will would be essentially redundant if we remembered all the answers too quickly. We're here to learn certain vital gross material lessons which cannot be acquired on higher planes of existence. The earth plane was designed to possess extreme polar opposites of positive and negative... as with the earth itself... and of course, an element of chaos is required by necessity. God is NOT what mankind has been duped into believing. If God were the ocean... WE are the drops of which it consists. Nothing is greater or lesser than yourself... we are separated merely by our intent and levels of Spiritual understanding. A lifetime is no different than a day at school... with volition to progress being paramount. Its spiritual simplicity is actually complicated to you... ONLY for now. As I said before, time is perceptual illusion. Please, now follow me Jonathan... all will become clear sooner than you may imagine!"

Sir Sébastien then turned and walked to a large arched baroque door which Jonathan had hitherto not noticed.

Astonishingly, the door proceeded to open without contact.

Following him as requested, they continued through into a long, narrow passageway leading to a similar looking arched doorway with walls which appeared to shimmer with some undefinable material... vibrantly coruscating throughout its entire length.

The dreadful inertia of Jonathan's earthly existence had recently become unbearable, but now, that awful sense of oppression was lessening with every step he took down this mystical and wondrous corridor.

Upon reaching the second door, Sir Sébastien paused for a brief moment just prior to it too opening in a similar manner to the first. What lay beyond the threshold of this particular doorway was beyond mere words to describe. The entire aperture was filled with a substance

which appeared akin to that of the Sun's neon photosphere... but with a more golden liquid-like undulating plasma layer rather than the illusory orange colour our three-dimensional physical eyes perceive.

The primary feature of this quintessence was its mirror-like effect... one's reflection could be clearly delineated and discerned.

With a comforting backward glance, Sir Sébastien entered through it... with almost terpsichorean grace.

Following a sharp intake of breath, Jonathan closed his eyes tightly and replicated the procedure, albeit with lesser finesse.

All fears and concerns vanished immediately as he stepped through the translucent 'portal' into an astounding room of empyreal beauty.

"You are now standing within an Arcturian inter-dimensional craft Jonathan," proclaimed Sir Sébastien with obvious exuberance.

Awestruck but still somewhat bewildered, Jonathan gazed, almost child-like, at the magnificence of his new surroundings.

"It's unimaginable... utterly, utterly unimaginable," whispered Jonathan, softly.

The craft was constructed of a material possessing pulchritudinous translucent radiant pastel shades appearing almost organic, which gave it a 'living' quality.

The Arcturians see life in all things emulating from the One Source.

Sir Sébastien, again smiling compassionately at Jonathan, endeavoured to explain about the craft as simply as he could.

"These craft are only seen by those to whom the Arcturians wish to reveal them... as they exist on a higher vibrational frequency and dimension. Understanding this high frequency of vibration is the key to understanding the mechanics of the craft. Propulsion is derived from the use of light crystals which are able to convert light energy from the solar centres... and transmutate that energy into power. These crystals have forces that can channel energy as massive as our Sun... and propel the ship for millennia. The craft is equipped with a room that can only be described as a grand database of the galaxy. The Arcturian knowledge of the galaxy and its inhabitants is extremely extensive and their stores of knowledge are kept within this room. Another room... very similar to the energy contained in this room... is the communications room. The Arcturians use these two rooms in combination with one another to communicate with other Arcturians and other races through what we would refer to as telepathy. In addition to these two rooms... the craft has many command rooms for navigation, living quarters, recreation... and even a room where any crew member can be transported back to the Arcturian home planet... in his etheric body."

"Are they peaceful... do they use weapons?" Jonathan inquired, worriedly.

"Arcturian craft are equipped with advanced shielding and defence mechanisms… but additionally, they ARE equipped with a form of weaponry, however, not as we might think of it. The Arcturian weapon systems have the ability to completely eliminate a target. The weapons cause no pain but have the ability stop reptilian and grey alien attacks. The Arcturians understand that all creatures and races must return to the One Source eventually… although war is absolutely, the last resort! Arcturian beings have a specific mission to assist humanity into the next level of ascension… and, with this goal in mind… there is the Soul room… which can be thought of as a hospital in which Arcturians are able to assist the energy of Souls in need… and revitalise them for their next learning experience. Here the Arcturians are able to assist those individuals who are ready to raise their vibrational frequencies into the next stage of development. An understanding of this magnificent craft would allow one to comprehend one's mission here on earth… as well help our fellow beings… and progress into higher stages of spiritual development and awareness. In time of doubt Jonathan… be reminded of the Arcturians ever watchful eye!" **Replied Sir Sébastien. Jonathan appeared as bemused as ever.**

"I still don't really understand… WHO and WHAT exactly ARE the Arcturians?" **he asked.**

"Arcturians are the highest, most advanced civilisation in the galaxy Jonathan… they exist mostly on a spiritual plane subjugated by thought and pure consciousness. The central belief system that sustains them is a philosophy of healing and compassion for the universe… and they teach that the most fundamental ingredient for living in the fifth dimension… is Love. Negativity, fear and guilt must be overcome and exchanged for Love and Light. Because they ingest energy rather than food, they are able to sustain their bodies through meditation… and this also eliminates the need for sleep and other limiting functions that Human, Grey, and Reptilian bodies experience. They work in close connection with ascended masters… whom they call the Brotherhood of the All. They also work closely with what they refer to as the Galactic Command. They are the most loving and non-judgmental beings you can possibly imagine. They are to us, Spiritual, mental, and emotional healers. We have not been hosts to a violent extraterrestrial attack here on Earth because most civilisations fear the advanced Arcturian ships," **relayed Sir Sébastien.**

"I still don't really understand… WHO and WHAT exactly ARE the Arcturians?" **inquired Jonathan.**

"Arcturians are between three to four feet tall, are generally slim and have a greenish hue about their skin… and very pronounced, almond shaped black or brown, eyes. They have the ability to, telekinetically, move objects with their minds. Their hands, unlike human hands, have only three digits. They can live anywhere up to four

hundred years... age slowly... and do not fall prey to sickness... as this was eradicated long, long ago. In the Arcturian civilisations, professions and life's paths are chosen by one's Spiritual level. This is used to decide which female is suited to give birth. The birth process itself is unlike that of ours... as it consists of a female and male mentally bonding... and thus a clone of the bond is produced as a result. Arcturus evolution is based on teachings of Spirituality... and so, as one evolves, one becomes more Spiritual. If one fails to reach his allotted goal, that individual is then tutored more... so the individual CAN succeed." **answered Sir Sébastien.**

"Is Arcturus the planet they come from?" **queried Jonathan.**

Delighted by the enthusiastic curiosity now being displayed, Sir Sébastien replied with a heightened degree of pleasure and satisfaction.

"The Arcturians originate from a crystal blue planet orbiting the star Arcturus... which is a red super-giant located in the constellation of Bootes. Arcturus is also the brightest star in that constellation... and lies thirty-six light years from Earth. The Arcturian world actually once existed in our third-dimensional plane and resembled our planet Earth... being abundant in oceans, rivers, forests and mountains. This is why Arcturians are so interested in our planet and our race... because they see THEIR past in our civilisation!"

"I still don't understand why I'm involved here?" **Jonathan probed.**

"Indeed... well... there's the rub my friend... YOU, as I was once myself, are unaware as to your true self and purpose... and thus, must be aided in remembering WHO you really are... and WHY you are here!" **elucidated Sir Sébastien with unashamed relish.**

He continued :

"There is a book which I have been instructed to entrust to your care in the hope that you will use its contents to help those on this third-dimensional earth plane who may be ready to ascend to the next level of existence... as ONLY those particular Souls will resonate to the true meaning of its words."

"A BOOK!" **blurted Jonathan.**

"Yes... a book... a very special book... a book which contains within its verses... the KEY to all of Creation!" **retorted Sir Sébastien, with utmost confidence.**

Suddenly, another burst of golden–white light then briefly blinded Jonathan once again.

As he slowly removed his hand from his eyes... he could see before him a shimmering metallic pedestal surmounted by a somewhat relatively small, simple, but nevertheless strikingly bound, iridescent, emerald green coloured book.

"I ask that you please read the words of 'Talium'... whilst here in this chamber!"

bade Sir Sébastien with gentle benevolence.

Puzzled, but curious, Jonathan approached the pedestal, hesitated for a few seconds, then proceeded to open the book.

Its pages appeared semi-transparent and had the texture of fine silk; the first being inscribed with an aureated appellation in Sumerian cuneiform script… followed by translations in various other languages:

Book of Divine Truth

Liber de Divino Vero

Incwadi Yeqiniso Waphezulu

Leabhar Dhiaga Fírinne

Llyfr Gwirionedd Dwyfol

Buch der göttlichen Wahrheit

Книга Божественной Истины

Βιβλίο της Θείας Αλήθειας

መለኮታዊ እውነት መጽሐፍ

ईश्वरीय सत्यको पुस्तक

Basahon sa Balaang Kamatuoran

Boek van de goddelijke waarheid

Bók guðdómlega Truth

წიგნი სალომრთო ჭეშმარიტების

Книга на Божествената Истина

ঐশ্বরিক সত্য কিতাব

神の真理の書

မြင့်မြတ်သောအမှန်တရား၏စာအုပ်

Գիրք Աստվածայֻֆ ձշմարտուֆյան

Incwadi kaThixo inyaniso

كتاب الحقيقة الإلهية

神聖的真理之書

దైవ ట్రూత్ బుక్

หนังสือแห่งความจริงของพระเจ้า

ספר של אמת אלוקית

Kitabu cha Ukweli Divine

Кніга Бажэственнай Ісціны

الہی سچائی کی کتاب

28

PART THREE

~ THE AFTERGLOW ~

Upon completing his reading of the book... Jonathan admitted to Sir Sébastien that he felt overwhelmed by profound bewilderment.

"Don't be too concerned Jonathan," he replied. *"You may not consciously realise it at this time... but you have already begun the re-awakening process. The book is so written that the words respond to attuned thought waves, releasing the associate mental vibrations of an exhilarating rhythm in the mind of the reader... thus, its magnanimous wisdom is ultimately revealed. Even your cursory reading of it will have glimpsed the thrilling beauty of its rhythm on a subconscious level. The Truth-seeker, who is willing to give them more intensive study, will open avenues to the most intrinsic wisdom... wisdom of unutterable majesty and beauty. YOU, as I am myself, are an Arcturian Guardian. You are loving, forthright, intense and typically, intolerant of abuse, dishonour, secrecy, dishonesty... and disloyalty. Throughout universal evolution... guardian races attempted to awaken humanity to the reality of its evolutionary destiny. All of the major Earth religions were seeded at one time or another by guardians, to help the races prepare for their eventual ascension. Though the teachings are often quite different or seemingly contradictory... and ALL religions have suffered manipulation and distortion at the hands of man and covert intruder extraterrestrial forces... they are united through their original purpose of achieving ascension and freedom from the illusions of matter. WE were created as a Guardian species... as planetary Guardians. We were created to stand as equals with the highest among the extraterrestrial races. In fact, we were created as a vessel through which digressing races could merge their consciousness and take on a new form that would give them the codes which would allow them to go through full transmutation out of time and matter. The Guardian Alliance is a very special group. One of the most noticeable things about them is that*

it's an inter-dimensional, inter-time group which comes from the future... 5260 A.D. as I understand. They came to help us here, because WE are their past. They are coming to CHANGE the past. Certain members of the Guardian Alliance are human... THEY are the original humans, the Turaneusiams (Children of the Lighted Ones). *They are taller than we are... and some of them are about twelve feet tall. They are very beautiful physically, compared to what our race is right now, with this mixed gene coding... plus they have abilities which we would look at as God-like. We are part of a HUGE group Jonathan... I believe there are over ten million races represented in our organisation alone... and that organisation is part of a bigger organisation called the Inter-dimensional Association of Free Worlds."* **explained Sir Sébastien, with profound sincerity.**

"I feel as though I'm the middle of a crazy lucid dream Sir Sébastien!" **said Jonathan facetiously, despite his increasing acceptance of the entire experience.**

"What happens now... do I get to meet these Arcturians?" **asked Jonathan cautiously.**

"I'm afraid... not at this juncture Jonathan... this entire craft is but a hologram... but in time you will... I promise. For now, please take the book and follow me once more," **said Sir Sébastien, in his consistently serene tone.**
Jonathan acquiesced without further question.

In a corner of the room suddenly appeared a gloriously beautiful blue corridor of light which opened to a golden round platform.
As soon as they entered the corridor, another room became visible.
A series of small golden steps led to its entrance.
The room was round and platinum in colour.
Upon entering, Jonathan could see stars and planets through a transparent domed ceiling. Inside the room was a reclining chair made out of what seemed to be solid crystal. It could also change colour.
In front of the chair was a large screen with a round dial. The dial was marked with the number twelve being in the centre. To the left of twelve... the numbers decreased... and to the right they increased.
Sir Sébastien told Jonathan that this room was a holographic healing chamber and that great healing and purification could be experienced here.

"Please sit in the chair Jonathan," **gently requested Sir Sébastien.**
As he positioned himself on the chair, Jonathan was amazed at how comfortable it was. Not hard as he had expected, but rather, incredibly soft.

The chair reclined itself to a forty-five degree angle.

The screen then became alive and was apparently driven by Jonathan's thoughts. At first it was scrambled and muddled. Sir Sébastien told him to go no further until he could control the screen in a calm and grounded way.

He disturbingly became aware of his body lying on the vestibule floor of Ravensbrooke Hall... and of being in the chamber at the same time. Over a few minutes... a harmonising sound was heard and he felt aware of both places.

The screen now had a beautiful geometry spinning in and out of form. Sir Sébastien asked Jonathan if he wanted to bring back lost or dis-associated energy. Irregardless of not quite understanding... he said yes. He was then asked to slowly turn the dial to the left.

He had only dialled back to the number nine when a series of 'energy discs' appeared on the screen... lined up as far as he could see into it. From time to time a disc would leave the line and float above... forming a small pile. After a time there was a pile about four inches high of silver discs that looked just like traditional compact discs.

Jonathan felt that there were now 'others' in the room.

A beautiful sound was toned and a beam of light from his third eye (or pituitary gland) and heart... was unified and sent to the small pile of floating discs. Instantly he felt a download from the discs and was aware of a flow of energy which felt comforting and welcoming.

The floating discs now began to slowly return to the spaces they had previously held in the line. After the last one was in place the whole line appeared to shuffle from right to left.

Sir Sébastien explained that our lives consist of many holograms layered upon each other... and here in the hologram... the holding of the energy from those discs would now change any experience or event that was in front of... or behind it.

The 'crystal' chair now began to gently spin to the left and the sounds of colours became like a rainbow.

Jonathan could feel every cell in his body being lit with this energy and light.

Gradually... the chair stopped and began to spin to the right.

He was shown that this would align this energy with his physical three-dimensional body that was currently in an, induced, tranquil and meditative state.

Their time was now complete in the chamber.

Sir Sébastien helped Jonathan up from the chair and back on to his feet... whilst telling him to send a mental beam of light from his 'Higher Heart' to his physical heart... in preparation for returning this fifth-dimensional energy back to his three-dimensional form.

No sooner than this was done, Jonathan found himself back in the dark vestibule of Ravensbrooke Hall.

Astonished... yet unafraid, he realised that he was hovering over his physical three-dimensional body like a gentle mist.

In his mind he could see the face of Sir Sébastien smiling with reassuring warmth.

The energy from Jonathan's fifth-dimensional experience appeared as 'the Book' transmuting into a liquid... which then poured into the top of his physical three-dimensional crown... filling every cell and crevice within his body.

Everything immediately went dark for several moments.

Jonathan opened his eyes as he lay on the cold vestibule floor.

His body felt strangely warm, but also heavy and clumsy.

As the energy integrated within him... he slowly regained his strength until normal function was resumed.

As he rose to his feet he could see that the large entrance door to the Hall... which had earlier closed shut... was now once again open.

Dusting himself down, Jonathan sighed as he looked around for the Book... without success.

It was gone.

With epiphanic clarity, he realised that he had somehow assimilated it into his very essence.

A tremendous sense of euphoria and confidence he'd never before experienced... permeated his entire being.

He knew that his quest for hope, purpose and inspiration was at an end.

As Sir Sébastien had promised... ALL had indeed become clear.

Snow was now falling as Jonathan slowly exited Ravensbrooke Hall. Closing the door behind him... he turned and looked up at the shimmering crystalline snowflakes as they drifted gently from the sapphire moonlit heavens.

Jonathan soliloquised as he walked in contemplation across the sparkling white cobblestoned forecourt to his car.

Before driving off... a wave of sadness flowed over him as he looked back at the enigmatic edifice... thinking of his incredible experience and the benevolent countenance of his guide... and brother, Sir Sébastien de Ravensbrooke.

It quickly passed, as he instinctively knew they'd meet again.

This was merely the beginning of the rest of his life in this holographic and illusory world... and a prelude to those... yet to be lived!

34

Truth is within ourselves; it takes no rise

From outward things, whate'er you may believe

There is an inmost centre in us all

Where truth abides in fullness.

~ Paracelsus ~

ROBERT BROWNING
1812 ~ 1889
English poet and playwright

Epilogue

We have the ability, each one of us on a spiritual level, to time travel... and to create ANYTHING without technology.

The reason we can do that is because of who we are and because of our extremes of emotion.

It is the male aspect of ourselves that creates the thought and the feminine aspect of ourselves that makes things manifest through that emotion.

Third density is incredibly dense and many extraterrestrial races don't like to extend their visits here. A good example about density resistance is if you moved your hand through a bathtub of glue.

That is how third density is experienced by some of the more evolved races.

Everything in our universe, including us, came from a black hole.

There is no age to us.

We are infinite.

Thus, what we do in life... TRULY DOES... echo in eternity!

Appendix

THE BOOK OF THE SACRED MAGIC
of
Abra-Melin the Mage

The Abra-Melin operation involves a period of withdrawal from society, focused daily prayer and meditation, and a number of other moral guidelines similar to those found in Monastic traditions around the world. It's broken down into progressive phases of increasingly diligent practice. The text advises against regarding the hour, day or month, or other socially-rooted habits. It also forbids the practice of any other system of magick that may be in any way contrary to the Abra-Melin Operation. In the Mathers translation from the incomplete French version, the phases last for two lunar cycles, each for a total of 6 months. In the original translation, the phases are much longer, the whole operation totalling 18 months.

You'll want to read the original text of the book in its entirety. There are sections on what should be considered before undertaking the process, as well as ritual specifications for building an altar and other ceremonial objects.

First Phase :
Ritual washing in the morning before sunrise, followed by a prayer for visitation from the Holy Guardian Angel, in a designated space with an open window and altar. Prayers are repeated after sunset. Maintain moderation in all activities, from food and drink to business and social affairs. Change the sheets and perfume the bed chamber on the eve of every Sabbath. Maintain purity, honesty and humility in all actions. Dress moderately, and always be willing to give to others.

Second Phase :
Continue morning and evening prayers, but ritually cleanse your hands and face with pure water before entering the altar space. Prayers should be prolonged and intensified. The whole body should be washed every Sabbath eve. All instructions of cleanliness and fairness from the first phase must remain, and ideally be strengthened in daily practice. A fast should be undertaken every Sabbath eve. A retreat from society should be made whenever possible, for as long as possible, during this phase.

Third Phase :

Prayers and ritual cleansing continue in morning and night, with the addition of a noon prayer session. All business operations should be ceased except those of charity. Perfume should be kept upon the altar. All free time should be dedicated to meditation, or the studying of sacred texts. All of society, except members of the household, should be shunned during this period.

After the Holy Guardian Angel is successfully invoked, individual spirits are conjured and bound.

While these summaries are oversimplified, this general framework has been adapted and altered by many practitioners throughout history. Some take a fundamentalist approach, believing that the ritual actually achieves the conjuration of supernatural entities and the acquisition of divine powers. The text warns, however, that only those with good intention may successfully complete the operation. Modern commentators often describe the Abra-Melin Operation as a sort of prolonged contemplative retreat. Diligent, repetitive practices like this can have a profound effect on programming the consciousness, and the transformative process can be unpredictable.

Overall, this practice, which calls for right conduct, action, livelihood, study, rigorous periods of meditation and social withdrawal, has some similarities to esoteric Buddhist and Hindu schools of thought.

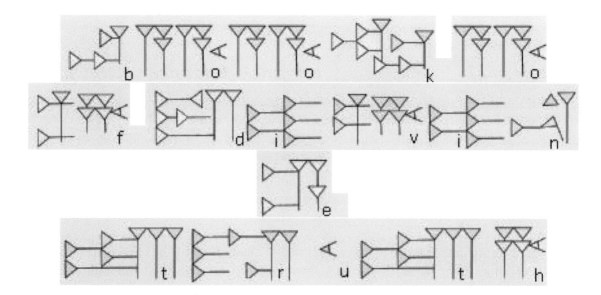

Bibliography

i. Hermes Trismegistus, (ed) Tabula Smaragdina, translated by Maurice Doreal, 1925.

ii. Lisa Renee, (ed) Shifting Timelines, Energetic Synthesis, 2015.

iii. Samuel MacGregor Mathers, (ed) The Book of the Sacred Magic of Abra-Melin the Mage, 1900.

Acknowledgements

We gratefully acknowledge the help and guidance of

all those who assisted our endeavour;
but particularly the following :

Helen Frances Graham;
Dennis Adne Graham;
Peter Baker;
Jonathan Christopher James Graham;
Lesley-Anne Graham;
The Kearney Family;
Angela Murphy and Lesley Hood;
John Molloy;
Ronnie Petrie and Doc Masson;
Shaun Murdanie Molloy and Elaina Rose Kelly;
Dan McMullen and Shannon Kelieff;
Holden Hunter and Heather Lohoar;
Paul Hugh McDermott, Jack Belcourt and Lewis Rutherford;
Rosa Mitchell;
Trish Torz;
Robert McHardy and the McHardy Family;
The Brady Family;
Steve Delaney and Dave Plimmer;
John Tams and Barry Coope;
Jackie Crowe and Willow Clifton;
The Spalding Family;
The Staff of St. Thomas' Primary School, Arbroath;
Nick and Chris Hill;
Scott Learmonth, Rhys Gourlay and Simon Kelly;
Henry Hogg Booksellers of Montrose;
The Royal Burgh of Montrose;
The Mount Cyrus Estate;
The Village of St Cyrus

✠ About the Authors ✠

Barry Dominic Graham was born in a small Benedictine convent hospital in

Winnipegosis, Manitoba, Canada... on land belonging to the Cree Nation Reserve.
He is of Scots/Irish ancestry.
He grew up in Glasgow, Scotland where he attended St Brendan's Primary School, Yoker;
Corpus Christi Primary School, Knightswood; then St Thomas Aquinas Secondary
School, Jordanhill (as did some notable others, such as the actor, James McAvoy; singer, Justin Osuji and
soccer player, Tosh McKinlay).
Over the years he has lived in Canada in several British Columbian locations, namely
Hope, Abbotsford, and Kelowna, as well as Prince Albert in Saskatchewan.
His son, Jonathan, lives and works in British Columbia, Canada.
He now resides in Montrose with his wife, Helen and their daughter, Hannah.
He is founder, director and author of the Montrose based 'George Beattie Project'.
His interests include: writing, nature, history, philosophy and Truth-seeking.

Hannah Helena Graham was born in Glasgow, Scotland.

She now resides in Montrose with her parents, Barry Dominic and Helen Frances
Graham.
In Montrose she attended Southesk Primary School and currently attends Montrose
Academy High School.
Her interests include: writing, nature, acting, singing and design.

"All matter is merely energy condensed to a slow vibration.
We are all one consciousness experiencing itself subjectively.
There is no such thing as death;
life is only a dream, and we are the imagination of ourselves. "

William Melvin Hicks
American philosopher, comedian and musician
1961 ~ 1994

By the Same Authors :

Mister Cumphobiecack
The Glumpet of Gleigh

Barry Dominic Graham
and
Hannah Helena Graham

Mister Cumphobiecack
And
The
Leprechaun's
Ball

Barry Dominic Graham
and
Hannah Helena Graham

Illustrated
by
Helen Frances Graham

A Very **Cumphobiecack** Christmas

Barry Dominic Graham
and
Hannah Helena Graham
Illustrated
by
Helen Frances Graham

The
Mister Cumphobiecack
Trilogy

Printed in Great Britain
by Amazon